Save the Ocean Fairies

By Daisy Meadows

www.rainbowmagicbooks.co.uk

The Fairyland Palace
GALA
FAIRYLAND ROYAL AQUARIUM
Fairyland Royal Aquarium
Kirsty's Gran's House
Lighthouse
The Park
Rockpool
Ocean Star Sailing Ship
Lea-On-Sea
Whales

Jack Frost's Ice Castle
Ocean World Sealife Centre
Seals
Dolphins
Baby Turtles
Leamouth Pier
Penguins
Ice floes
South Pole

Contents

Story One:

Ally the Dolphin Fairy

Story Two:

Pia the Penguin Fairy

Story Three:

Tess the Sea Turtle Fairy

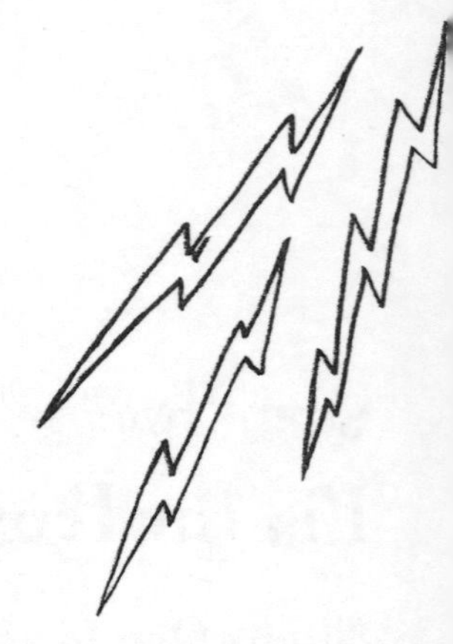

Jack Frost's Spell

The Magical Conch Shell at my side,
I'll rule the oceans far and wide!
But my foolish goblins have shattered the shell,
So now I cast my icy spell.

Seven shell fragments, be gone, I say,
To the human world to hide away,
Now the shell is gone, it's plain to see,
The oceans will never have harmony!

Story One
Ally the Dolphin Fairy

Chapter One
Off to Fairyland

Kirsty Tate and Rachel Walker stepped off the bus and blinked in the sunshine. The two girls were staying with Kirsty's gran in Leamouth for the spring holiday and today they'd come to Lea-on-Sea, a small seaside resort along the coast. "I've got some shopping to do, so I'll meet you

back here at midday," Kirsty's gran said, getting off the bus. "Have fun!"

"We will," Kirsty assured her. "See you later, Gran." Then she turned to Rachel. "Come on, let's go down to the beach!"

It took the girls just moments to walk down the sandy steps to the curving bay, which was packed with families enjoying the sun. The sky was a clear, fresh blue, and a breeze ruffled the tops of the waves. Lots of children were swimming in the sea, while shrieking seagulls soared above them, their strong white wings stretched wide.

"It's lovely," Rachel said, slipping off her shoes and wiggling her bare toes in the warm sand. She pointed to the far edge of the bay. "Let's go over there, shall we? It's a bit less crowded."

The girls made their way across the beach, zigzagging between deckchairs, windbreaks and sandcastles. Then Kirsty stopped walking suddenly and bent down. "Hey, look at this shell," she said, picking it up to show Rachel. "It's really sparkly."

Rachel peered at the fan-shaped scallop shell, which was a creamy-white colour with pink edging. And yes – tiny golden sparkles were fizzling all over it!

Rachel's heart quickened with excitement as she looked at Kirsty. "That looks like fairy magic," she whispered.

"Just what I was thinking," Kirsty replied, smiling. "Oh! And I can feel something underneath it, too."

She flipped the shell over in her palm and both girls saw a tiny golden scroll tucked into it, tied with a pretty red ribbon. Rachel untied the ribbon and unfurled the scroll, then both girls leaned over to read the tiny writing there.

"King Oberon and Queen Titania hereby invite you to the Fairyland Ocean Gala," Kirsty read in a whisper. "Oh, wow!"

Rachel felt a rush of excitement. She and Kirsty had been to Fairyland many times now, and had enjoyed lots of wonderful fairy adventures, but the thought of visiting their fairy friends was always a treat. "What are we waiting for?" she said. "Let's hide behind these rocks so nobody sees us – and go to Fairyland!"

Once they were hidden from view, Rachel and Kirsty opened the pretty golden lockets they wore. The lockets had been a present from the fairy king and queen and contained magical fairy dust, which would transport the girls to Fairyland. Their fingers trembling with

excitement, the two friends each took a pinch of the sparkling pink dust and sprinkled themselves with it.

Instantly, a glittering whirlwind spun up about them, and they felt themselves shrink smaller and smaller to fairy-size. Kirsty just managed to grab Rachel's hand, as they whizzed around very quickly. Then, after a few moments, the whirlwind dropped and the girls felt themselves lowered gently to the ground.

"Another beach!" Rachel exclaimed in delight, gazing around. "A Fairyland beach!"

"And we're fairies!" Kirsty cried, fluttering the beautiful gauzy wings on her back, loving the way that they shimmered all the colours of the rainbow in the sunlight. The two friends were standing

on the beach next to the Fairyland Royal Aquarium, an unusual building made of glass and stone, and the Gala was in full swing. Hundreds of fairies were dancing to lively music, competing in fun swimming races, enjoying boat rides, and tucking in to the most wonderful-looking ice creams. "There are the Party Fairies," Kirsty said, spotting their old friends flitting about,

making sure that everyone was having fun. "Oh, and there's Shannon the Ocean Fairy!"

Rachel and Kirsty had met Shannon during a very special summer adventure, which had taken place last time they'd holidayed in Leamouth. Shannon was fluttering towards them now, followed by some other fairies the girls didn't recognise. "Hello Kirsty, hello Rachel!" Shannon cried happily. "It's lovely to see you again. These fairies are my Ocean Fairy helpers, who take care of the creatures in the Royal Aquarium – and throughout all the oceans, too!"

Shannon introduced the fairies – Ally the Dolphin Fairy, Amelie the Seal Fairy, Pia the Penguin Fairy, Tess the Sea Turtle Fairy, Stephanie the Starfish Fairy,

Whitney the Whale Fairy and Courtney the Clownfish Fairy.

"Hi," said Whitney, who was wearing a brightly patterned dress. "Have you been to one of our ocean parties before?"

"No," Kirsty replied. "But this one looks great! Are you celebrating something special?"

"We hold a Gala like this every

summer," explained Tess, who had long blonde hair in two plaits. "It's lots of fun, but important too. Shannon plays a tune on the Golden Conch Shell which ensures peace and harmony throughout the ocean for the whole year. It's up there, look."

Tess was pointing at a small stage in front of the Aquarium, with a table in the middle, covered in a midnight-blue velvet cloth. On top of the cloth sat a large golden shell, which glittered with magic.

"Talking of which … it's about time I began," said Shannon. She winked at Rachel and Kirsty. "Wish me luck!"

As Shannon walked onstage, a hush fell over the party. "Good afternoon, everyone," Shannon said in her tinkling voice. "I hope you're all having a lovely time at our annual Ocean Gala."

"No!" came a bad-tempered voice just then. "No, I am not having a good time, actually!"

Rachel's mouth fell open in shock as a grumpy-looking figure barged through the crowd and onto the stage. "Jack Frost!" she hissed. "What's he doing here?"

Kirsty bit her lip. Horrid Jack Frost was such a trouble-maker! "I don't know," she replied in a whisper, "but it looks like we're about to find out."

Chapter Two
Shattered!

"Excuse me …" Shannon said politely, but Jack Frost grabbed the microphone and began addressing the crowd.

"I hate the ocean!" he ranted. "I can't swim, and I detest getting sand between my toes. It's no fun for me, so I don't see why I should let you lot enjoy yourselves.

Lads – to work!" he ordered.

At his words, a group of five goblins rushed onstage and grabbed the Golden Conch Shell, hurrying away with it before Shannon or any of the other Ocean Fairies could stop them. But in true goblin style, they immediately began arguing about which way to go, and who was going to carry it.

The goblins pulled the shell back and forth between them until, as a result of their struggles, it suddenly flew high into the air … and smashed to the ground, breaking into pieces.

Shannon ran over to collect the pieces

of the broken shell but Jack Frost was too fast for her.

"*The shell may be shattered, but I don't care. I'll scatter its pieces everywhere!*"

he chanted, waving his wand at the fragments of shell. A blast of icy magic burst from his wand, spiralling and whirling around the seven broken pieces and sending them flying into the air. Then, they were gone.

"Your precious shell is scattered all over the human world now," Jack Frost sneered. "You'll never find the pieces and your ocean world will be forever in chaos!"

Then, with another wave of his wand and a horrible cackle of laughter, he and his goblins vanished from sight.

Shannon had turned very pale. "This is awful," she said anxiously. "Until I can play the Golden Conch Shell, the ocean will be in a terrible state! All the creatures will be confused – they won't be able to find their homes or families. What are we going to do?"

Queen Titania stepped onto the stage and put a comforting arm around Shannon. "Don't worry," she said. "I can't stop Jack Frost's spell, but I'll do my best to alter it. Come, let us go to the Royal Aquarium, and I'll explain my plan. Ocean Fairies, you come too," she said. Then her eyes fell upon Kirsty and Rachel and her serious expression softened. "Hello, my dears," she added. "Would you join us, as well? We need your help again."

Kirsty and Rachel both bobbed curtseys. "Of course," Kirsty said politely.

They followed the queen into the huge entrance hall of the Royal Aquarium, which had a polished marble floor, and lots of glass tanks arranged along one side. The windows at the top of the hall were made of stained glass, and featured pictures of different sea creatures – mighty whales,

leaping dolphins, dainty seahorses, and many more. Sunlight streamed through them, casting colourful reflections onto the floor.

The glass tanks varied in size, and each housed a single creature: a dolphin, a seal, a penguin, a starfish, a turtle, a whale and a clownfish. All seven creatures were surrounded by faint golden sparkles,

Kirsty noticed.

"This is my plan," Queen Titania announced. "These are the seven Magical Ocean Creatures who are the companions of our Ocean Fairies. I now proclaim them the guardians of the seven pieces of the Golden Conch Shell." She waved her wand and a jet of silver magic burst from its tip and swirled around the Aquarium.

The light from the magic was so bright, Rachel had to shut her eyes – and when she opened them again, the tanks were empty. The Magical Ocean Creatures had gone!

"Where are they all?" dark-haired Ally gasped, peering at the tank where her dolphin had been swimming just moments earlier.

"Where's Echo?"

"I have sent all seven creatures out into the human world," the queen said. "They will become the right size for the world, and will find themselves near a piece of the Golden Conch Shell. My fairies, your job is to find the Magical Ocean Creatures once again, and each collect a piece of the shell."

"We'll help," Rachel said, feeling a rush of excitement at the thought of another fairy adventure.

"Thank you," the queen said, smiling at Rachel and Kirsty. Then she turned to Ally. "I will send you out first," she declared. "Kirsty and Rachel will help

you look for Echo. Good luck!"

She pointed her wand at Ally, then at the two girls, and a glittering whirlwind immediately lifted them off their feet and spun them up into the air.

Chapter Three
Where's Echo?

When Kirsty and Rachel landed, they were back to their usual sizes, and were standing outside a building called 'Ocean World'. "It's a sea-life centre," Kirsty realised, reading a nearby poster. "This says 'See the ocean creatures, with our amazing underwater tunnels and the unique ocean-

side stadium'. Perfect!"

"Echo must be inside somewhere," Ally said from where she was fluttering near Rachel's shoulder. She looked rather like a glittering butterfly, with her beautiful long silver dress and sparkly wings, Kirsty thought. "Come on, let's go in."

Kirsty's gran had given the girls some spending money and luckily they had just enough to pay the entrance fee, so in they went, with Ally tucking herself into Rachel's pocket so that she'd be out of sight. As they walked through the Aquarium, they couldn't help noticing that the ocean creatures were acting very strangely. "Look," Rachel said in surprise, stopping in front of one glass tank filled with tropical fish. "These angel fish are turning somersaults!"

Kirsty stared. Sure enough, the pretty striped fish were swimming loop-the-loops in the water – and looked very dizzy!

Then, further along, they saw three catfish in a tank who were tickling each other with their whiskers, and some octopuses whose tentacles were all tangled together in knots.

"This is awful," Ally said, looking

worried. "And it's all because Shannon didn't get to play her tune on the Golden Conch Shell. We've got to find the pieces to put the conch together again as soon as possible."

Just then, an announcement came over the tannoy system. "Ladies and gentlemen, our wonderful Wild Dolphin Show is about to begin – please take your seats in the ocean-side stadium!"

"Dolphins?" Kirsty said excitedly. "Echo might be there. Come on!"

The girls and Ally quickly made their way to the ocean-side stadium. It was an open-air arena with a wonderful view down to the sea. A wooden jetty had been built close to the water, and the girls saw some boys in Ocean World uniforms there, carrying buckets of fish.

A couple of dolphin trainers strode on to the jetty and waved at the audience. "Hi, everyone!" one of them called. She had a blonde ponytail and a big smile. "Welcome to the Ocean World Wild Dolphin Show, where you're going to see dolphins performing some amazing tricks."

"These dolphins are wild dolphins, who live freely in the ocean," said the second trainer, a man with short brown hair. "But they love showing what they can do – and they love their dinner too!" He grinned and threw a handful of fish into the sea, and immediately a group of dolphins appeared, swimming gracefully in and out of the water.

"I love the way they look like they're

smiling," Rachel said, her eyes glued to the beautiful creatures.

"Me too," Ally said, peeping out of her hiding place in Rachel's pocket. "But I can't see Echo anywhere," she added, sounding disappointed.

"For our first trick, the dolphins are going to jump through this hoop," the first trainer announced, showing the audience a bright red hoop. "They love doing this – just watch!" She held the hoop out above the water expectantly but the dolphins didn't seem interested. In fact, they completely ignored the trainer and her hoop.

The trainer looked a bit embarrassed.

"Hey, guys," she coaxed the dolphins, waving the hoop around. "Over here!"

Ally shook her head. "Oh dear," she whispered. "This is because the Golden Conch Shell is missing, I know it. The dolphins look really confused."

It soon became clear that the dolphins

didn't want to jump through the hoop, or balance beach balls on their noses, or do any tricks at all. "I'm really sorry, everybody," the man with brown hair said, "but we'll have to cancel today's show. I don't know what's wrong with the dolphins – they usually love performing!"

A sigh of disappointment went up from the audience, and people got to their feet to leave. Rachel stood up too, but Kirsty grabbed her hand to stop her. "Wait," she said. "Look at those boys."

Rachel and Ally peered down to see what Kirsty had noticed. The two boys who'd been carrying the buckets of fish were messing about on the jetty now, throwing fish at each other. One boy's cap fell off, and the girls and Ally gasped as they saw what a pointy nose the boy had

… and what green skin, too!

"They're goblins!" Rachel realised, her stomach lurching at the sight. What were they doing there?

"Oh no," Ally cried. "Jack Frost must

have realised that Queen Titania changed the spell. He's sent his goblins into the human world to get the missing shell pieces before we do!"

Chapter Four
Goblins Underwater

The three friends fell silent. This was terrible news! They couldn't let the goblins find the missing shell pieces first. But then Ally spoke again, and this time she sounded much more cheerful. "Oh look, there's Echo! Do you see that sweet little dolphin following the others?"

Rachel and Kirsty peered down at the sea. The group of dolphins were heading away from the stadium, and behind them swam a small, pretty dolphin, whose silvery coat sparkled in the sunshine. "The piece of shell must be somewhere nearby," Kirsty realised. "We've got to get in the water and go after her."

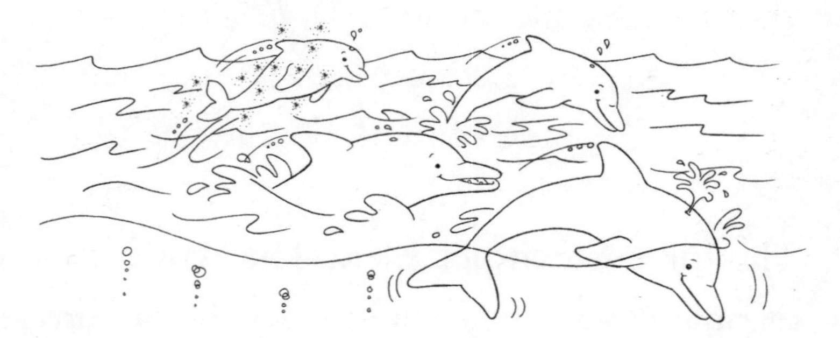

Ally smiled and a dimple flashed in her cheek. "No sooner said than done," she declared. She waved her wand and silver sparkly fairy dust flowed around Kirsty and Rachel, turning them into fairies

again! "Now you need one of these each," she said, waving her wand again and conjuring up two magic bubbles. The bubbles settled over the girls' heads, like diving helmets, then disappeared with a pop. Rachel and Kirsty knew from their adventures with Shannon that they would now be able to breathe underwater, and that they would stay warm and dry!

"Ready? Let's go!" said Ally. Then the three of them flew to the sea and plunged into the water after Echo and the other dolphins. Rachel grinned at Kirsty as they swam through the cool clear water.

What an adventure this was turning out to be!

The three fairies followed the dolphins deep into the ocean, all the way to a beautiful underwater grotto, full of colourful sea anemones and waving fronds of seaweed. Ally gave a high whistle, and Echo turned her head.

At the sight of her fairy mistress there in the grotto, Echo made a happy clicking sound and swam over at once, looking delighted to see her. Ally gave Echo a hug and stroked her silvery nose. "Hello there," she said, smiling. "Have you seen the piece of Golden Conch Shell anywhere?"

Echo shook her head. "I've asked the other dolphins, but they just seem really confused by everything," she replied. "I haven't searched this grotto yet though. Maybe we can do that together."

The friends swam further into the cave and began looking all over for a piece of the Golden Conch Shell.

"There's something glittering down there," Kirsty said excitedly, pointing at one corner of the cave floor. "I wonder if it might be the shell?"

But just as they were about to go and take a closer look, Ally hissed a warning. "There are divers heading this way," she said. "Hide!"

She, Kirsty and Rachel immediately darted behind a large clump of seaweed so that the divers wouldn't see them. The girls knew that the existence of the fairies had to be kept a closely guarded secret from other humans.

The two divers swam closer. The light was dim down in the ocean but Rachel

couldn't help noticing what big feet they had – so big, in fact, that they had no need for flippers. Then she realised that the divers' skin looked rather green-ish, too …

She elbowed Kirsty. "They're goblins!" she whispered. "And I think they've seen the shell!"

Chapter Five
A Sparkling Shell

Rachel was right. The divers were goblins – and they were heading straight for the sparkling piece of shell that lay in the corner of the cave. "Quick!" Kirsty cried. "We've got to get there first!"

The three fairies and Echo swam as fast as they could towards the shimmering

piece of shell – but before they or the goblins could reach it, a small pink crab scuttled over and picked up the shell piece in its pincers.

"That's definitely part of the Golden Conch," Ally said in excitement, as sparkles of light streaked through the water from the shell. "Come on!"

Before the fairies could get there, though, the goblins reached the crab, and one of them held out his hand. "Give it here, Stalk-Eyes," he ordered rudely.

The little crab held tight to the shell, and some other, bigger crabs emerged from behind a rock and formed a protective circle around their friend, snapping with their pincers to keep the goblins away.

"How can we get rid of those goblins?" Rachel wondered, as one of them made a grab for the piece of shell. She turned to

Ally. "Could Echo and the other dolphins chase them away, do you think?"

Ally smiled. "You bet," she said, and whispered something to Echo. Echo nodded, her mouth falling open in a smile, and she made a series of clicks and whistling sounds to the other dolphins.

Immediately all the dolphins rushed towards the goblins, who looked absolutely terrified at the sight. "Don't eat me!" cried one. "Help! Swim for your life!"

"Aaaarrrghh!" screamed the other goblin. "Mummy!"

The frightened goblins turned and swam off as fast as they could. Rachel grinned

from ear to ear. She loved it when a plan worked out!

"Now we just need to persuade the little crab to play swapsies," Ally said thoughtfully, picking up a small stone from the seabed. She waved her wand and a stream of silvery lights danced through the

water from the wand, and all around the stone ... turning it into a gleaming white pearl!

Ally swam over to the crab.

"Look at this beautiful pearl," she said, holding it out to show him. "Would you like to swap it for that piece of broken shell?"

The crab dropped the piece of Golden Conch Shell at once and picked up the pearl, looking very excited.

"Thank you," Kirsty smiled, reaching out to take the piece of shell.

"Look out!" Rachel shouted suddenly,

as the goblins, followed by Echo and the other dolphins, careered back into the grotto. The goblins and dolphins were going so fast that they caused a current of water to surge through the cave – which lifted the piece of shell right off the seabed and sent it whizzing away from the three fairies.

Kirsty made a lunge, but before she could grab the piece of shell, a goblin

snatched it up and swam quickly out of the grotto.

"After him!" called Ally. "Don't let him get away!"

Chapter Six
Catch that Goblin!

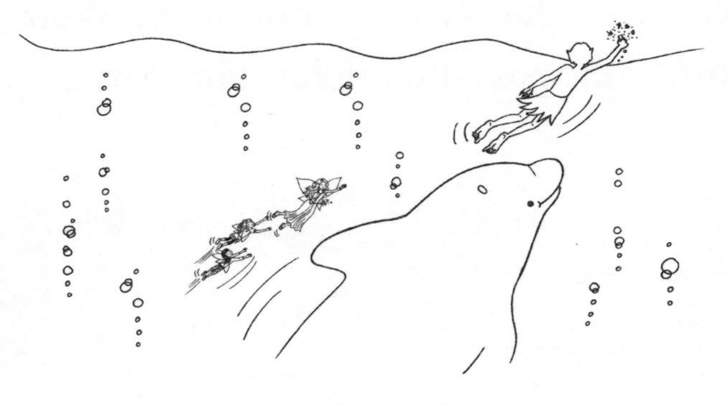

Kirsty, Rachel, Ally and Echo immediately gave chase. The goblin swam all the way up to the surface and, as the others followed, they suddenly heard a lot of noise. Once their heads broke the surface of the water, they realised why.

"It's a water-skiing display!" Kirsty cried

in alarm, swerving to avoid a speedboat that roared past her. All around them were speedboats whizzing along, towing water-skiers behind them, and up on the beach, a crowd was watching the action.

Just then, the girls saw one water-skier zoom right past the goblin who was

holding the piece of Golden Conch Shell. He stretched out a hand and grabbed the piece of conch as he whizzed by … and they realised that he was a goblin too.

They watched in dismay as he zoomed away at a tremendous speed. "We're never going to catch up with him," Rachel said. "There's no way we can swim that fast."

"No," said Ally, "but the dolphins can, can't they?" She grinned and leapt out of the water and onto Echo's back, taking hold of the strong fin. Then she gave a whistle and two other dolphins swam over to Kirsty and Rachel. "Ladies – your carriages await," Ally smiled. "Jump on board!"

Kirsty and Rachel didn't need telling

twice! They both fluttered out of the water and onto their own dolphins, clinging tight to their fins. "And off we go," Ally cheered. "Come on, Echo!"

Echo and the two other dolphins surged through the sea, and Rachel almost fell off her dolphin's back in surprise. It was going so fast – she felt as if she were flying!

Great cheers of excitement went up as

the spectators on the beach spotted the dolphins, and the three fairies hunched low by the animals' fins, not wanting to be seen. The dolphins were closing in on the water-skiing goblin. Then, suddenly, all three of them leaped out of the water at once, making the goblin jump in surprise.

The startled goblin lost his balance and tumbled into the sea ... dropping the piece of Golden Conch Shell as he fell!

"Oh no!" he yelled in dismay, his arms

flailing as he tried to catch it. Echo was too quick for him, though. With another deft leap into the air, she caught the piece of shell in her mouth and dived back into the water.

The other two dolphins that Kirsty and Rachel were riding on followed, and, once they were all a safe distance from the goblins, the girls slipped off their backs.

"Thank you," Kirsty said, patting her

dolphin's silky body. "I enjoyed that so much."

Meanwhile, Ally was hugging Echo, delighted to have the piece of Golden Conch Shell. "Well done, Echo," she said happily. "And well done, Kirsty and Rachel! I'd better take Echo and this piece of shell back to the Fairyland Royal Aquarium

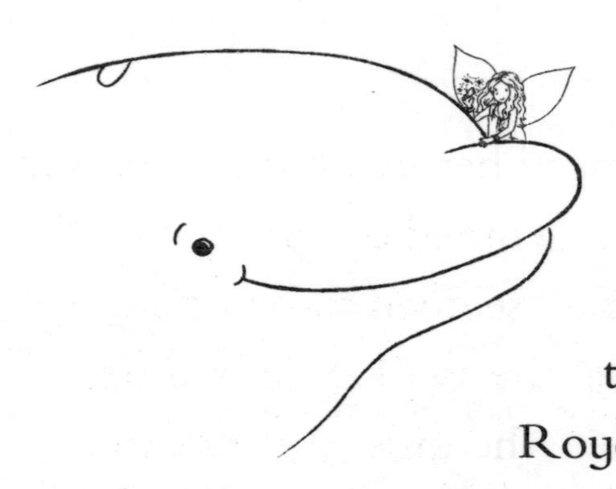

now, but I'm sure we'll meet again. I'll send you two back to your world – thanks for everything!"

Kirsty and Rachel hugged the smiling fairy, and Echo, too. They would never forget their wonderful dolphin adventure!

Then Ally waved her wand and a stream of silver sparkles whirled around them all, so that everything seemed to blur before their eyes. When the sparkly whirlwind died down again, the girls were back on the beach at Lea-on-Sea, behind the very same cluster of rocks where they'd started their fairy adventure.

"We've only been gone a minute," Kirsty said as she looked up to check the time on the clock tower. Then she smiled

at Rachel. "That was the most exciting minute of my life, I think."

Rachel was smiling too, as she gazed out at the waves tumbling onto the shore. "I can't wait for our next ocean adventure," she said. "I think we're in for a very magical holiday!"

The End

Story Two
Pia the Penguin Fairy

Chapter One
Ice to See You!

"Wheeee! This is fun!" squealed Kirsty Tate, whizzing along on roller skates. "Race you to that tree, Rachel!"

Kirsty's best friend, Rachel Walker, grinned and sped along even faster on her skateboard. "No worries," she called out breathlessly, just overtaking Kirsty at the

last moment. "The winner!" she cheered, slapping a hand to the trunk of the old oak tree a split-second before Kirsty did.

The two girls laughed. It was a sunny spring day and they were on holiday together in the seaside resort of Leamouth, staying with Kirsty's gran for a whole week. Today they'd come out to Leamouth Park, which was at the top of Leamouth Cliffs, overlooking the sea.

"Doesn't the water look

pretty with the sun shining on it?" Kirsty commented dreamily, staring out at the ocean below them. It was a perfect blue, with thousands of twinkling lights dancing on the surface from the sun, and just a few ruffles of white where a breeze was whipping up the waves.

"I know," Rachel agreed. "It's so sparkly, it almost looks magical." Then she grinned at Kirsty. "Talking of magic, I hope we meet another Ocean Fairy today!"

"Me too," Kirsty said. "We're so lucky to be friends with the fairies, aren't we?"

"The luckiest girls in the world," Rachel agreed happily.

She and Kirsty had had lots of fairy adventures together so far, and at the start of this week, they'd fallen straight into another – this time with the Ocean Fairies. The girls were helping the Ocean Fairies look for the seven broken pieces of their Magical Golden Conch Shell, which kept the ocean world in order. Each piece of the shell was being guarded by the fairies' animal helpers, so the hunt was on to find them!

It had been horrid Jack Frost who had ordered his goblin servants to steal the Magical Conch Shell at the Fairyland Ocean Gala party. The clumsy goblins had ended up breaking the shell, though, which had caused all sorts of problems

throughout the oceans. Now the broken pieces of shell were scattered across the seas in the human world, and the girls and their fairy friends were trying to find them all before the goblins got their hands on them again.

Kirsty and Rachel set off along the path once more, and before very long, Kirsty heard a tinkling tune drift over to them.

"Is that an ice-cream van?" she asked hopefully, feeling hungry at the thought. Her gran had given them some spending money, and it

seemed a long time since breakfast all of a sudden.

"Yes!" Rachel said, whizzing further down the path and spotting the colourful van parked up near the playground. It was still playing the jaunty tune while a large plastic ice cream rotated on the roof of the van. "Come on, let's go over and have a look."

The girls zoomed up to the van and gazed at the pictures of ice creams on the side. A friendly-looking man with a white cap on his head leaned out

of the hatch. "What can I get you, girls?" he asked.

"Orange crush, double choc pop, strawberry fizz … Ooh, how are we going to choose?" Kirsty said, licking her lips as she read. "What do you fancy, Rachel?" she asked. Then, when her friend didn't reply, she turned to her. "Rachel?"

Rachel didn't seem very interested in the list of ice creams, though. She was staring excitedly up at the roof of the van where the plastic ice-

cream cone was still turning.

And, as Kirsty looked up at it too, she realised why. Perched on top of the revolving plastic cone was a tiny smiling fairy, waving down at them. It was Pia the Penguin Fairy!

Pia had coffee-coloured skin and glossy black hair which was piled up on her head and fastened with a red bow. She wore a black and white polka-dot dress with a wide red belt around the middle, and red pumps with black bows on her feet.

"What's it going to be, then?"

the ice cream man asked. "Have you decided?"

"Um … no," Rachel said, unable to drag her eyes away from Pia as she fluttered off the plastic cone and hovered in mid air like a sparkly butterfly. The tiny fairy gestured to the girls to follow, then flew gracefully into a bush behind the ice-cream van. "Actually, I'm not that hungry after all," she said, smiling apologetically at the ice-cream man. "Maybe later. Thanks anyway!"

She grabbed Kirsty's arm and they walked towards the bushes where they'd seen Pia flying.

"Over here!"

they heard Pia's silvery voice call, and then Kirsty noticed a faint shimmer in the air, above one large flowering bush.

Feeling tingly with excitement, Kirsty and Rachel checked that nobody was looking, then sneaked behind the large bush, where they saw Pia sitting on a leaf and smiling at them. "Hello again," she said. "I'm so pleased to see you two. I've got a feeling I know where Scamp,

my little penguin, is, and I'm hoping he's guarding a piece of the Magical Golden Conch Shell. Will you help me look?"

Kirsty and Rachel didn't need to be asked twice. "Of course!" they said.

A dimple flashed in Pia's cheek as she smiled again. "I was hoping you would say that," she replied, and waved her wand through the air. "Let's go!"

Chapter Two
Let it Snow

When Kirsty and Rachel had been at the gala party in Fairyland, they had learned that each of the Ocean Fairies had a special magical animal helper, who lived in the Royal Aquarium. After Jack Frost had made the broken pieces of the conch shell disappear, the Fairy Queen had used

her magic to send the magical creatures out into the human world after the shell pieces.

If the Ocean Fairies could find their animal again, they would know that a piece of the shell was nearby. So far, the girls had helped Ally the Dolphin Fairy and Amelie the Seal Fairy find their magical creatures as well as two pieces of the conch shell. But where would little Scamp the penguin be – and where was the third piece of the shell?

There was no time to think about that now though, because fairy magic was streaming from the end of Pia's wand and wrapping

Kirsty, Rachel and Pia in a sparkly whirlwind that lifted them off the ground and spun them away at breath-taking speed.

"Whoaaa!" Kirsty squeaked. "This is even faster than my skates!"

After a few moments, the girls felt the whirlwind slow. Then their feet touched the ground once more, and they were able to look around.

"Wow," Rachel said, blinking in surprise. "Snow!"

"Lots of snow," Kirsty said in delight. It felt as if they'd landed in a winter wonderland, with soft white snow blanketing every surface.

They were standing at the edge of the shoreline, but it felt a million miles from the beach at Leamouth, with its twinkling blue sea. Here, the sea was full of floating ice floes and there was a freezing wind sweeping in from the water.

Luckily, Pia's magic had changed the girls' clothes from the shorts and T-shirts they'd been wearing

before, and they were now wrapped up snugly in thick snowsuits, hats, boots and gloves, feeling lovely and warm.

"Oh, look," Rachel gasped, pointing ahead. "Polar bears! Aren't they amazing?"

"Polar bears – ahh, we must be at the Noth Pole, then," Kirsty said, feeling pleased with herself for remembering.

Pia shook her head, looking worried. "No – this is the *South* Pole," she said. "Oh dear,

the polar bears shouldn't be here! This is all because the Golden Conch Shell is missing. Everything's topsy-turvy in the oceans right now – it's even affected creatures who live near the oceans, like the polar bears."

"Well, there are some penguins at least," Rachel said, pointing to a group of the distinctive black and white birds who were huddled together on an icy patch near the

water's edge. "Can you see Scamp among them, Pia?"

Pia fluttered high into the air and scanned the crowd of birds. "Not from here," she replied. "Let's take a closer look."

The girls and Pia made their way across the snow towards the penguins. As they drew nearer, Kirsty noticed that some of the taller penguins had something tucked under their feathers above their feet, which they occasionally fussed over with their beaks. "What are they doing?" she asked Pia curiously.

Pia smiled. "They're the daddy penguins," she replied, "and they're looking after the eggs by keeping them warm on their feet. It's a very

important job."

Rachel watched one proud father penguin checking over his particular egg with his beak – but unfortunately he was rather too energetic about it. The next thing she knew, the egg had rolled right away from the penguin and was skidding over the slippery ice towards the sea.

"Oh no!" cried Rachel, breaking into a run. "We've got to catch that egg!"

Chapter Three
Ready, Steady, Hatch

The egg was heading right for the water and the girls hurried as fast as they could towards it. It was so difficult to run on the slippery snow, though!

"If only we had our skates and skateboard," Kirsty cried helplessly, skidding on some ice and almost falling over.

"Good thinking," Pia told her, waving her wand. A flurry of blue sparkles streamed from its tip all around the girls and in the very next second, a pair of ice skates appeared on Kirsty's feet, and a snowboard was under Rachel's.

"That's more like it," Rachel whooped, whizzing over the snow and catching the egg just before it plopped into the sea.

"Well done, Rachel," Kirsty said, skating up to join her. "And, look, here comes Daddy to collect it."

She and Rachel went to meet the daddy penguin who was waddling anxiously towards them. "Here you are," Rachel said, carefully setting the egg on the penguin's big black feet. "No damage done."

But then she heard a faint tapping sound and looked down to see that the egg had cracked right across the middle. "Oh no!" she cried in alarm. "It is broken after all."

Pia, who'd flown over, landed lightly on the egg and

inspected it. Then she looked up at the girls, her eyes sparkling. "Don't worry," she told them. "That crack is meant to be there. The chick inside is hatching out."

"Oh!" Kirsty cried excitedly. "What perfect timing! And now we get to see a newborn baby penguin – how brilliant!"

Pia laughed at the delighted look on Kirsty's face. "Not so fast," she warned. "It can take the babies a little while to break out of their eggs. This one might not hatch for

some time."

But just as she was speaking, another, longer, crack appeared in the egg.

"Come on, little penguin," Rachel said encouragingly, crouching down. "You can do it!"

Tap, tap, tap, went the penguin chick from inside the egg.

"He's tapping away at it with his beak," Pia explained, as yet another crack

appeared on the surface. This was the biggest crack so far. "Actually, I think we might just see him any second now..."

Crack! The eggshell broke clean in two and there sat a fluffy grey chick about the size of a tennis ball, with soft pink feet and tiny flippers.

"Oh my goodness," Kirsty breathed, unable to stop smiling. "That is just the cutest thing I've ever seen in my life!"

"Totally cute," Pia agreed, as the daddy penguin bent down to guide the baby out

of the egg for a cuddle. "But now we really should be … what's that noise?"

They turned at the sound of shouts, and a roaring engine. A snowmobile was approaching – and riding on it was a group of people, all bundled up in bobble hats and scarves. But they weren't just ordinary people, Rachel realised, as she noticed what long green noses they all had …

"Oh no," she said. "The goblins are here! They must be looking for a piece of the

conch shell, too."

"And they're really upsetting the penguins," Pia said anxiously, trying to calm a nearby daddy penguin who was looking very worried by the noise of the snowmobile.

The other penguins seemed startled and jumpy by the goblins' arrival too,

and huddled closer together to protect their eggs. Meanwhile, some of the other penguins walked away from the huddle, flapping their blunt flippers and making snapping sounds with their beaks.

"What are they doing?" Kirsty asked Pia, confused.

"It looks like they're trying

to cause a diversion," she replied. "I think they're hoping to lead the goblins away from the new chick and the eggs." Then she gasped. "And there's Scamp – right at the front of the group. Maybe he knows where the shell is!"

"Follow those penguins!" Rachel cried at once, setting off after them on her

snowboard. "If Scamp has found the next piece of the conch shell then we've got to get to it before those goblins do. Come on!"

Chapter Four
Trying Flying

The goblins had also noticed the group of penguins waddling away, and immediately turned their snowmobile around so that they could chase after them. "Hey, they're sneaking off!" the girls heard one of the goblins shout eagerly. "Maybe they know something about the missing conch shell.

Come on, lads!"

"One of them is very sparkly, too. Look," a second goblin added, narrowing his eyes as he stared. He pointed at Scamp. "I bet he's got something to do with that shell! After them!"

Vrrrooom! went the snowmobile as it zoomed along, sending a shower of snow spraying up on each side as it went.

The penguins, meanwhile, were moving very strangely, flapping their wing-like flippers and taking little hops into the air before landing on their tummies and sliding along the snow.

Rachel stared as she followed them. "Are they trying to fly?" she asked Pia, baffled. "I didn't think penguins could."

Pia, who was perched on Kirsty's shoulder, looked just as surprised as Rachel. "They can't usually fly,"she replied. "But they seem to think they can now!

Everything's topsy-turvy because the Golden Conch Shell's been broken." She sighed. "If only the goblins hadn't smashed it before Shannon the Ocean Fairy could play the special tune on it, none of these strange things would be happening!"

"Still, the penguins are going pretty fast," Kirsty commented. "They're managing to keep ahead of the goblins at least."

But just then, the goblins roared forwards even faster on their snowmobile – and one of them leaned out daringly and made a grab for Scamp.

"Oh no!" Pia cried out anxiously. Then she gasped with relief. "Just missed him – thank goodness!"

"Knowing what goblins are like, they're sure to try again though," Rachel said. "We've got to stop them. Let me think …"

Kirsty giggled. "I've got an idea," she said suddenly, as she whizzed along on her skates. "Pia, do you think you'd be able to magic up a big snowman in front of the goblins? It would startle them, and hopefully make them slow down."

Rachel grinned. "Yes!" she said. "Maybe the snowman can be holding up a stop sign, like lollipop ladies do near schools? The goblins are so silly, they might even think it's a real person – like a lollipop snowman!"

Pia's dimples twinkled in her cheeks as she smiled. "That's a great idea," she agreed. "One lollipop snowman ... coming up!"

She waved her wand, and a stream of pink sparkles whooshed out of it. A split-second later, a gigantic snowman, glittering with fairy magic, plopped down a short distance in front of the snowmobile. And yes, he was carrying a stop sign. Only instead of saying 'Stop! Children Crossing' like a lollipop lady's sign, it said 'Stop!

Penguins Crossing'!

"STOP!" yelled the goblins to the driver, all looking alarmed at the sight.

"Whoa!" the goblin driving the snowmobile yelped, swerving to a halt. The penguins, meanwhile, carried on their funny flying-sliding-waddling and managed to get further away across the snow.

"Hang on a minute," one of the goblins

said, peering at the snowman. "Why is it all sparkly like that?" He glanced around and then spotted Rachel and Kirsty whizzing up behind them. "Oh, right. Pesky girls and their fairy friend – that's why the snowman is sparkly. They just magicked it up here!"

The goblins stuck their tongues out at the girls and drove around the snowman, before chasing after the penguins again.

The penguins were now half-sliding and half-flying down a steep slope. Rachel blinked as they suddenly disappeared from view. "Where did

they go?" she yelled in alarm, trying to slow down. But the slope was so steep, she found herself going faster and faster down it. "I can't stop!" she shouted in fright.

"Neither can I!" called Kirsty, who, in her panic, had completely forgotten how to slow down on ice skates. "And I think this is the edge of a cliff!"

The goblins were shouting too. "Use the brake! Use the brake!" the ones in the back yelled to the driver. "Stop!"

"Turn sideways!" Pia called to the girls. "Now!"

Rachel and Kirsty turned as hard as they could, and luckily both managed to stop just in time, right on the cliff edge. "Phew," Rachel breathed, panting and feeling shaky. "That was close."

The goblins, meanwhile, had managed to stop the snowmobile, but the driver had braked so sharply, they'd all been flung right out of it, and were now tumbling down the slope, gathering snow as they went.

"It's a goblin snowball," Kirsty said, her eyes wide at the sight of the huge white ball, with green arms and legs sticking out of it, all waving furiously. "And it's heading straight for us!"

"They're going to knock us over the cliff!" cried Rachel.

Chapter Five
A Crystal Cavern

Quick as a flash, Pia waved her wand. Sparkling fairy dust billowed around the girls and then, just as the goblins were about to crash into them, Kirsty and Rachel felt themselves shrinking down smaller and smaller ... and then gossamer wings sprouted on their backs. They were

fairies again!

Down tumbled the goblins off the cliff and up fluttered the three fairies, in the nick of time! "Phew," gasped Kirsty, her heart thumping at the close escape. "Thank you, Pia."

Pia was busily waving her wand again, though. "Much as those goblins annoy me, I'd better give them a soft landing," she explained, and the girls saw a huge drift of soft powdery snow appear beneath the

falling goblins.

Plop! Splat! Splurge!

The goblins dropped into the snowdrift and sank. Snow flew everywhere as they scrabbled to get out, their arms and legs waving wildly.

"Let's leave them to it and fly after the penguins," Rachel suggested. "I can't see them anywhere now, can you two?"

"No," Pia said, looking around. "Let's swoop down low. We might be able to pick up their trail."

The three friends soared over the cliff,

their hair streaming back in
the wind as they flew.
Once they were
closer to the
ground,

Kirsty spotted some distinctive penguin footprints.

"They're heading this way!" she called, pointing ahead. "Come on, let's follow them."

At first sight, the footprints seemed to lead straight into an icy wall, but as the fairies flew nearer, they realised that the 'wall' was actually the entrance of an icy cavern.

The big snow-covered archway that led to

the cavern was almost invisible against the pure white landscape.

"Ugh, my feet are so cold and wet," Rachel heard the goblins grumbling. She turned quickly to see that they had all clambered out of the snowdrift and were looking very grumpy.

"Quick, let's fly inside the cavern," she said in a low voice, not wanting the goblins to notice them.

Pia and Kirsty agreed, and they all darted into the gleaming cavern. Glittering icicles hung from its roof, and the walls and ground were covered in thousands of twinkling ice crystals. "There's Scamp!" Pia cried in delight, flying over to a cute little penguin who was standing in the middle of the cavern.

"Hello!" he squeaked excitedly as he saw her, and waddled over to her at once. "It's up there," he said, gesturing at the ceiling with one of his flippers.

"So it is!" Rachel exclaimed, gazing up and beaming as she saw the sparkles shining from the ceiling. "The shell piece has been frozen into

one of the icicles!"

"Oh, clever Scamp," Pia said, kissing his cheek. "Well done for finding it. Now then, how are we going to get this down?"

She, Rachel and Kirsty flew up for a closer look at the shell-icicle. But before they could say another word, they heard stomping footsteps and in came the goblins.

"Aha! Fairies!" one of them said, pointing triumphantly. "And what's that they've found up there?"

"Ooh! Ooh! It's a piece of that magic shell!" a second goblin cheered.

The goblins whooped in delight. "Let's snowball it down!" one of them suggested, scooping up a handful of snow and packing it into a tight round snowball.

Splat! Splat! Splat! The goblins all copied their friend, throwing snowball after snowball at the icicle.

Kirsty, Rachel and Pia had to dodge out of the way as the icy balls whizzed towards them. "Hey!" Pia yelled. "Be careful! You don't want to break it!"

But the words had only just left her mouth when ... *Smash!* The icicle shattered and the shell piece went flying.

"Get it!" shouted the goblins.

"Get it!" cried the girls.

Chapter Six
Pop-up Penguin

Luckily, the piece of conch shell landed just near Scamp and he immediately tucked it under the fluffy feathers above his feet, just as Kirsty and Rachel had seen the daddy penguins protect their eggs. The goblins lunged towards Scamp but the other penguins, seeing what was happening,

huddled around Scamp to protect him.

"Out of the way, you lot," one of the goblins grumbled, trying to push through the penguins and receiving a few sharp jabs from their beaks for his rudeness.

"Ow! Stop pecking me! Ow!" he cried, rubbing his arm.

The other goblins were also being pecked by the penguins, who were determined to keep their friend Scamp safe.

"Where is Scamp?" Kirsty whispered from where they were hovering above the

black and white birds.

Before Pia could answer, Scamp's head popped up from the penguin huddle. "Catch me if you can!" he squawked cheekily.

"Grab him!" one of the goblins yelled crossly, still trying to push through the penguin crowd.

But moments later, Scamp popped up from a different part of the huddle and gave another playful squawk. "Can't catch

me!" he teased.

Pia giggled. "He's really winding those goblins up, isn't he?" she said. "But maybe I should get him out of there now ..."

Scamp popped up again and one of the goblins made a lunge for him. He was just about to grab hold of the little penguin when Pia quickly waved her wand, magicking Scamp and the shell to fairy-size, then flying in to snatch them up herself. The goblins grabbed wildly for Pia, but she managed to fly high enough so that she was out of

their reach.

"Let's get away from here," Rachel said, and the three fairies zoomed out of the cavern, with Pia holding Scamp and the shell piece close to her.

"We did it!" Pia cheered, cuddling Scamp tightly. "Well done, girls. Another piece of shell is safe – that's wonderful news."

"Not so wonderful for the goblins," Kirsty said, seeing them trudge out of the cavern below, looking very gloomy, and bickering about who was going to tell Jack Frost the bad news.

"No," Rachel agreed. "But the penguins seem happy. And look, they've stopped doing that strange trying-to-fly thing now."

Pia smiled as the penguins trooped out and waddled along the ice back to the sea. Once in the water, they began swimming and diving as normal. "I think it must be because we've found another piece of the shell," she said. "Bit by bit, the ocean is

returning to how it should be. Hurrah!"

She stroked Scamp's glossy feathers. "And now we should get the shell piece back to the Royal Aquarium in Fairyland, where it will be safe. Thanks for everything, girls!"

"Thank you," Kirsty said, hugging her. "That was fun!"

"Bye, Pia, bye, Scamp," Rachel said. "I loved seeing all the penguins – especially that little baby. So cute!"

Pia waved her wand and a flood of fairy dust streamed around Kirsty and Rachel, and instantly, they were spun into the air very fast in a glittery magic whirlwind. Moments later, they found themselves back in Leamouth Park, and they were girls once more, and back in their summery clothes with their roller skates and skateboard.

One thing was different though – they were each holding a huge cone, filled with pink and white scoops of ice cream and

covered in edible sparkles!

"Yum!" Kirsty said in delight, taking a big lick of hers. "Delicious!"

Rachel grinned and licked hers too. "Tastes magic to me," she said. "What an *ice* way to finish an adventure!"

The End

Story Three
Tess the Sea Turtle Fairy

Chapter One
A Magical Sandcastle

"Shall we build another tower, Kirsty?" Rachel Walker asked her best friend, Kirsty Tate.

The two girls were kneeling on the beach, making an enormous sandcastle. They'd been working on it all day in the sunshine. The castle had turrets and towers

and archways.

"Oh, yes, brilliant idea!" Kirsty said with a grin. She picked up her bucket. "Let's start decorating the castle, too. We can use those pretty pink and white shells we found earlier."

Carefully, Rachel began to build the tower. Meanwhile Kirsty tipped the shells out of her bucket and began sorting through them.

"Look, Kirsty, the sun's starting to set," Rachel pointed out, noticing that people were packing up and leaving the beach. "We'll have to go back to your

gran's soon." The girls were spending the spring school holiday in Leamouth with Kirsty's gran.

Kirsty's face fell. "I know we've had a lovely time on the beach, Rachel," she sighed, "but we haven't seen a single magical fairy sparkle all day! I was hoping we were going to find another missing piece of the Magical Golden Conch Shell."

"Me, too," Rachel agreed. "But don't forget what Queen Titania always says – we have to wait for

the magic to come
to us!"

On the first day
of their holiday, the
girls had been thrilled
to receive an invitation
to the Fairyland Ocean
Gala. There they'd met their old friend, Shannon the Ocean Fairy, as well as the other Ocean Fairies and their Magical Creatures. The highlight of the gala was to be the moment when Shannon played the beautiful Golden Conch Shell. This would make sure that there was peace, harmony and order in all the oceans of the world for the next year.

But before Shannon had a chance to play her magical tune, Jack Frost and his goblins had burst onto the scene. On Jack

Frost's orders, the goblins had grabbed the Golden Conch Shell, but as they argued over it, the Conch Shell had fallen to the ground and smashed into seven shining pieces.

Jack Frost had immediately raised his ice wand and, with a burst of freezing magic, he'd scattered the seven fragments in different hiding places throughout the human world. Shannon, Rachel, Kirsty, and all the fairies had been horrified. They knew that without the Golden Conch Shell, there would be chaos and confusion in the oceans.

"It doesn't look like any magic is going

to come to us today, though," Kirsty remarked. She began pressing rows of tiny, creamy shells onto the sides of the sandcastle. "But at least we've helped the Ocean Fairies find three pieces of the Golden Conch Shell so far."

"And we know that four of the Magical Ocean Creatures are still guarding the four missing pieces," Rachel pointed out.

Luckily, Queen Titania had acted quickly to limit the power of Jack Frost's spell. The queen had used her own magic to send the Ocean Fairies' Magical

Creatures out into the human world to guard the shell fragments until they were found and returned safely to Fairyland. Then the Golden Conch Shell could magically repair itself and Shannon would be able to play it at last.

"Isn't our castle great, Rachel?" Kirsty said proudly, sitting back on her heels to take a look. There was hardly anyone left on the beach now besides the two girls.

Rachel nodded. "It looks a bit like the Fairyland Palace with all those towers," she replied. "Except our castle isn't so sparkly, of course!"

Suddenly Kirsty gave an excited cry. "Are you sure, Rachel?" she asked with a big smile. "Look in there, under that archway!"

Rachel bent forward on her hands and

knees and peered inside the sandcastle. Then she saw it! A glittering, golden light was shining right in the very centre of the castle.

"Kirsty, I think it's a fairy!" Rachel gasped, spotting a tiny figure dancing gracefully through the sandy rooms. "It's Tess the Sea Turtle Fairy!"

Tess fluttered over to the archway and waved up at the girls. She wore cropped blue trousers and a pale blue sparkly T-shirt with an aquamarine cardi

over the top. Her silky blonde hair was braided in two bouncy plaits.

"Girls, I'm so glad to see you," Tess called in a silvery voice. "Come and join me inside your beautiful sandcastle!"

She pointed her wand at Rachel and Kirsty and a stream of sparkles swirled around them. The girls felt themselves shrinking as they'd done so many times before, and in the twinkle of an eye, they

were fairy-sized with gossamer wings just like Tess's.

Quickly, Rachel and Kirsty flew under the archway and joined their fairy friend inside the sandcastle.

"We're really pleased to see you, Tess!" Kirsty beamed at the fairy. "Have you found another piece of the Golden Conch Shell?"

Tess nodded. "I think so," she replied. "My magical sea turtle friend, Pearl, is guarding it. But it's far away from here in a tropical land. Will you come with me, girls?"

"Of course we will!" cried Rachel eagerly.

"Gran isn't expecting us home just yet," Kirsty added. "Let's go right away!"

Chapter Two
Turtle Trouble

Waving her wand, Tess flew around Rachel and Kirsty as they hovered in the air.

Immediately a dazzling cloud of fairy sparkles surrounded the girls. They closed their eyes and felt themselves whisked away from Leamouth beach, whizzing

through the air at a speed that took their breath away.

Suddenly the air felt much warmer. Rachel and Kirsty opened their eyes and saw that they were flying over a tropical beach. The ocean was a clear aquamarine colour, and the sand was a pure, soft white. Palm trees fringed the shore, their leafy fronds waving in the gentle breeze. It was dusk, like it had been in Leamouth, and the pink and gold sun was sinking slowly into the rippling water.

"Oh, isn't it beautiful?" Kirsty sighed happily. She peered down at the beach as it began to get a little darker. "I wish we'd got here a bit earlier so that we could see it all in the daylight."

Rachel was squinting down at the beach, too. "What are those?" she asked, sounding puzzled. "They look like little polka dots, but they're running around – and there are lots of them!"

At first Kirsty couldn't see what Rachel meant, but as her eyes adjusted to the dim light, she too could see little round shapes. They were scurrying across the sand in every direction.

"Let's fly a bit closer," said Tess, "and then you'll be able to see what they are!"

Curious, Rachel and Kirsty followed Tess as she floated down towards the beach.

"Oh!" Kirsty exclaimed suddenly. "They're baby sea turtles!"

"Aren't they cute?" Rachel laughed.

The little green turtles were using their tiny flippers to move across the beach away from the ocean. As the girls watched, they saw sand flying in all directions and more baby turtles began to appear from holes in the ground.

"Those are the ones that have just hatched," Tess explained. "The mother turtle buries her eggs under the sand."

"But why are all the baby turtles running away from the ocean?" Kirsty

asked, curious.

Tess sighed. "When baby sea turtles hatch, they should head straight for the water," she explained. "But the poor little things are confused, like the other ocean creatures, because all the pieces of the Golden Conch Shell haven't been found yet!"

Kirsty and Rachel shared an anxious glance.

"What will happen to them?" Kirsty asked. "Can we help?"

"Maybe we can carry them to the ocean and put them in the water," Rachel suggested.

"No, there are far too many!" Tess replied, glancing down at the hundreds of tiny turtles below them. "We must find Pearl. Then she'll be able to lead the babies safely to the ocean."

"Shall we fly around and look for her?" asked Rachel.

Tess nodded. "But stay close to the beach," she told them.

Rachel and Tess flew off in different directions along the beach. Meanwhile, Kirsty zoomed over to the palm trees and began to zigzag slowly between them, keeping a sharp lookout for Pearl. Suddenly

a loud voice coming from the treetops overhead almost made Kirsty jump out of her skin.

"My feet are cold and wet! I HATE having cold, wet feet!"

Kirsty froze in mid-air and glanced upwards, but she couldn't see anything. Quickly she whizzed back to the beach.

"Rachel! Tess!" Kirsty called to her friends. "Over here!"

"Have you found Pearl?" Rachel asked eagerly as she and Tess rushed to join Kirsty.

"No, but come and listen to this!" Kirsty told them. She led Rachel and Tess over to the palm trees. As they hovered there, they heard a shrill, complaining voice above them.

"My feet are cold and wet, too! There's

horrid, itchy sand between my toes!"

Kirsty glanced at Rachel and Tess. "Did you hear that?" she whispered. "Goblins!"

Chapter Three
Follow the Leader

Tess frowned. "It sounds like goblins," she replied. "We all know they don't like having cold, wet feet! Let's take a look."

Tess flew upwards, towards the voice, and Rachel and Kirsty followed. Suddenly they heard the sound of Tess's tinkling fairy laughter.

"Girls, these are the most handsome goblins I've ever seen!" she called.

Surprised, Rachel and Kirsty flew higher. Then their eyes widened and they too burst out laughing. Four beautiful scarlet and blue parrots were perched on the top of the palm tree. As Tess and the girls watched, one of the parrots opened his beak and squawked, "I hate sand!"

"I hate sand!" the parrot sitting beside him repeated crossly.

"The parrots are mimicking the sound of the goblins grumbling and arguing!" Rachel said with a grin.

"But that means there must be goblins around here somewhere," Kirsty pointed out.

Tess nodded. "So it's even more important that we find the missing piece of the Golden Conch Shell before the goblins do," she said anxiously. "I wonder where Pearl is? She's the only one who can help us."

"Let's carry on searching," said Rachel.

Tess and the girls flew off along the beach again, above the baby turtles who were still scurrying around. It was almost dark now, but there was a large pale

moon, and stars were beginning to sparkle in the midnight-blue sky.

"Doesn't the moonlight make everything look magical?" Kirsty remarked, staring out over the waves gently lapping the shore. Then she blinked, wondering if she was seeing things. Was that a golden glow out there on the water, glittering in the light of the moon?

"There's something shiny and sparkly in the ocean!" Kirsty shouted excitedly. "I think it might be a missing piece of the Conch Shell!"

Rachel and Tess gazed in the direction Kirsty

was pointing.

"It looks like the waves are carrying it to the shore," Rachel said, her eyes fixed on the sparkling glow.

"Come on, girls!" Tess cried, zooming off towards the water.

Rachel and Kirsty rushed after her and the three friends hovered in the air as the glowing object floated closer to the beach.

"It's not a missing piece of the Conch Shell," Tess exclaimed with delight. "It's Pearl!"

Rachel and Kirsty watched the magical green sea turtle swim gracefully through the waves and onto

the shore. Pearl's beautiful shell glittered with fairy magic as she pulled herself higher up the sand with her strong flippers.

"I'm so glad you found us, Pearl!" Tess flew down and stroked the turtle's head. "We need your help."

"Yes, the baby turtles are running away from the ocean, instead of towards it," Rachel explained.

"And we know there are goblins around here somewhere because the parrots are talking like them!" Kirsty added.

Slowly Pearl nodded her head, her dark eyes wise and kind. "The missing piece of

the Golden Conch Shell is around here somewhere, but I'm not quite sure where," she explained. "I saw it bobbing around on the waves, but then I lost sight of it. I think it might have been washed up on the shore."

"Maybe we should look after the baby

turtles first, and lead them safely to the water," Tess suggested. "I'm very worried about them. Then we can start searching for the shell."

Rachel glanced down at the beach below them. To her surprise, she saw that the baby turtles had stopped running aimlessly away from the ocean. Instead they were all scuttling along the beach, heading the same way in one big crowd.

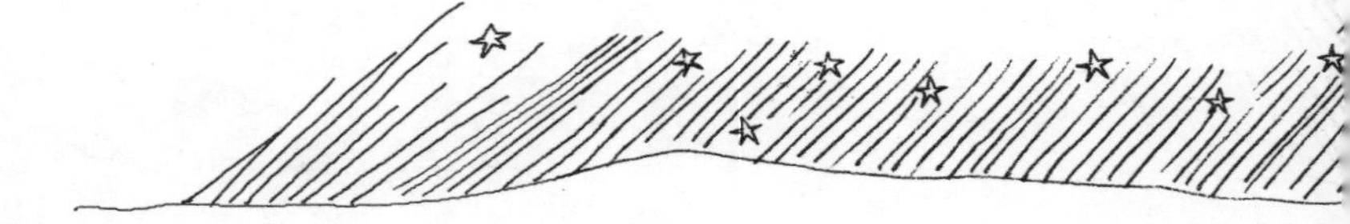

"What's going on?" Rachel wondered. Then, at the front of the crowd of turtles, she spotted a group of three children wandering along the beach. One of them was carrying a bucket. "Look," Rachel went on, surprised, "I think the baby turtles are following those children!"

"Let's find out," Tess said. She flew off with Rachel and Kirsty right behind her,

and Pearl followed them along the sand.

As Tess and the girls got closer to the children, they noticed something very odd.

"Why are they wearing big straw hats and sunglasses?" Kirsty whispered, frowning. "The sun's gone down, and it's dark!"

"Look at their footprints, too." Tess pointed down at the sand. "They have very big feet for children."

"And very big ears!" Rachel said in a low voice, spotting large, pointy ears sticking out of the straw hats. "They're not children at all. They're goblins!"

Tess, Kirsty and Rachel glanced at each other in dismay.

"But why are the baby turtles following them?" Kirsty asked, confused, glancing down at the large crowd of turtles still

scurrying along behind the goblins.

Tess grinned. "Well, the turtles have only just hatched," she replied. "And since they're green, and so are the goblins, the babies think the goblins are grown-up turtles!"

Chapter Four
Pogwurzle Panic

Rachel and Kirsty couldn't help laughing.

"I wonder if the goblins know they're being followed?" said Rachel.

"And I wonder what the goblins have got in that bucket!" Kirsty whispered.

Suddenly the biggest goblin happened to glance around and see the baby turtles. He

gave a shriek of fear and peered nervously down at the tiny creatures.

"Look!" the goblin yelled, squinting through the darkness. "We're being followed by – I don't know what they are!"

The other two goblins spun round.

"What are you so scared of?" the goblin with the bucket asked scornfully.

"They're only little, whatever they are. They can't hurt us!"

"They can if they're baby pogwurzles!" the

third goblin gasped.

All three goblins yelped with fright.

"Ooh, pogwurzles!" groaned the goblin with the bucket, backing away from the baby turtles. "I hate pogwurzles even more than I hate sand between my toes!"

"Shoo!" shouted the biggest goblin. He whipped his straw hat off and began flapping it at the baby turtles. The others did the same. "Go back to Pogwurzle Land!"

The baby turtles took no notice.

"They're going to attack us!" the goblin with the bucket shouted as the turtles came closer. "Run for your life!" And all three

goblins raced off along the beach in a panic, leaving the turtles behind them.

"After them!" Tess cried.

Tess and the girls dashed after the goblins while Pearl followed behind, keeping an eye on the baby turtles.

When the goblins spotted Tess, Rachel and Kirsty flying overhead, they scowled and ran even faster.

"Pesky fairies and scary pogwurzles!" the biggest goblin groaned. "Go away!"

Kirsty noticed that the goblin holding the bucket was looking very worried. He was gripping the bucket tightly with both hands, keeping it

very close to him.

"What's in your bucket?" Kirsty called as she, Tess and Rachel flew alongside the goblins.

"None of your business!" the goblin yelled. "I'm not telling you what we found—"

The biggest goblin skidded to a halt and immediately clapped his hand over the first

goblin's mouth.

"Keep your big goblin mouth shut!" he ordered angrily. "Those fairies are just trying to trick us into telling them that—"

Quickly the third goblin clapped his hand over the biggest goblin's mouth.

"Don't tell our secret, blabbermouth!" he shouted.

Furiously the biggest goblin slapped his hand away.

"Now the fairies and the pogwurzles know that we have a secret!" he snapped. "You've given the game away!"

"No, I haven't!" the third goblin retorted.

"They don't know that we found the—"

"Shut up!" the first and second goblins shrieked frantically. "Don't say anything!"

"I think there's a missing piece of the Golden Conch Shell in that bucket," Kirsty whispered to Rachel and Tess. "I'm going to take a look!"

As the goblins argued fiercely about what they should or shouldn't say, Kirsty flew towards the goblin with the bucket. But just as she was about to peep inside it, the goblin spotted her.

"Leave me alone!" he shouted, whisking the bucket away from Kirsty.

"Let's help Kirsty by distracting the goblins," Tess murmured

to Rachel, and they flew to join her.

"Be careful," Rachel called. "The baby pogwurzles are catching up with you!"

All three goblins moaned with terror as Tess and Rachel fluttered around them.

"The pogwurzles are going to nibble our toes!" the goblin with the bucket gasped. As he turned to glance at the baby turtles, who were getting closer again, Kirsty saw her chance. She flew down once more and this time she managed to get a glimpse inside the bucket.

Sure enough, there lay a piece of the missing Golden Conch Shell, glinting in the moonlight!

Chapter Five
Pearl and a Plan

Excited, Kirsty waved at Rachel and Tess.

"It's here!" she mouthed silently, pointing at the bucket.

The goblins hadn't noticed Kirsty this time. They were huddled together, staring in panic at the baby turtles, who'd also come to a stop as they waited for the

goblins to start moving again.

"We can't get away from these baby pogwurzles," the biggest goblin muttered. "They're going to follow us all the way back to Jack Frost's Ice Castle!"

"And then Jack Frost will be really angry with us," the third goblin added. "We need a plan to get away from them. Any ideas?"

"We could jump in the sea and swim away," the goblin with the bucket suggested.

"That's a great idea," said the biggest goblin eagerly. "Except we can't swim, you idiots!" the third goblin snapped.

As the goblins argued, Kirsty flew quickly over to Rachel and Tess.

"We need a plan, too!" Kirsty whispered. "How are we going to get the shell piece out of the bucket?"

"And how can we stop the baby turtles from following the goblins, and lead them back to the ocean?" Rachel added.

Tess's face lit up. "Pearl can help us do both!" she replied with a beaming smile. "Come on, girls!"

The three friends left the goblins arguing and flew along the beach a little way to where Pearl was waiting patiently.

Tess dipped down and whispered something to her. "Of course," Pearl agreed, nodding her head.

Rachel and Kirsty watched as Pearl began to move towards the baby turtles, pulling herself along the sand with her flippers. As Pearl got closer, her shell began to glow with dazzling fairy magic, as bright as the moon shining above them.

Slowly the baby turtles turned their heads to look at the glowing light of Pearl's shell. Then, losing interest in the goblins, they all turned and hurried towards Pearl instead.

"Look!" shouted the biggest goblin with relief. "The baby pogwurzles are going away!"

"Yippee!" yelled the other goblins, and they jumped up and down with glee.

"Let's go home to Jack Frost right away," the goblin with the bucket suggested. "He's going to be very pleased when he sees what we've found!"

The biggest goblin nodded. "Give me the bucket then," he said. "It's my turn to carry it."

"No, it isn't!" The goblin with the bucket hugged it protectively against him. "You can't have it!"

"Stop arguing, you two," said the third goblin. "I'll carry the bucket!"

The goblins were

so busy fighting over the bucket, they didn't notice that Pearl was now leading the crowd of baby turtles towards them.

Rachel, Kirsty and Tess watched as the baby turtles followed Pearl closer to the goblins. In just a few moments, the goblins were surrounded as the little turtles scampered around them.

Suddenly, the biggest goblin looked down and gave a yelp of fear. "The pogwurzles

have sneaked up on us!" he shouted. "We're trapped!"

"Help!" shouted the goblin with the bucket, letting go of the handle in panic.

As the bucket hit the sand, the glittering piece of the Golden Conch Shell fell out and rolled towards Tess and the girls. Instantly Rachel swooped down and picked it up.

"Those fairies have our shell!" the biggest goblin yelled furiously. "We must get it back!"

"We can't," groaned the goblin who'd dropped the bucket. "We're surrounded by baby pogwurzles!"

"Just a minute ..." The third goblin

frowned as he peered more closely at the baby turtles around them. The glow from Pearl's shell was lighting up the darkness, making the turtles more visible. "I don't think these are baby pogwurzles," the goblin announced at last. "They don't look scary at all. It's just another fairy trick!"

The goblins scowled at Rachel, Kirsty and Tess.

"Give our shell piece back!" the biggest goblin demanded.

Tess turned to Rachel and Kirsty.

"We have to take the shell back to Fairyland before the goblins can grab it," Tess said urgently. "But first we need to guide the baby turtles safely to the ocean!"

Chapter Six

Four Found, Three to Go!

Tess beckoned to Pearl, who nodded. The turtle hurried towards the ocean, her shell still glowing brightly, and the baby turtles began to follow.

Meanwhile Tess waved her wand around herself, Rachel and Kirsty as they hovered in the air. Suddenly a shimmering, silvery

light surrounded them.

"Now the baby turtles will follow us, as well as Pearl," Tess told the girls.

Bathed in the shining glow, Tess, Rachel and Kirsty flew towards the ocean.

"The turtles are coming!" Kirsty called with delight as she looked down and saw all the babies rushing towards the water.

"STOP!" the biggest goblin roared, chasing after Tess and the girls. "Give us the shell back!"

"She has it!" the third goblin yelled, pointing at Rachel as she flew past him.

"Let's grab her!"

"We can't reach her," the biggest goblin said with dismay. "There are too many of these!"

And he pointed down at the crowds of baby turtles at their feet. There were so many of them, they were creating a barrier between Rachel and the goblins. Rachel sighed with relief, clutching the shell piece more firmly.

The turtles were now slipping into the water and swimming away as Pearl, Tess, Rachel and Kirsty watched over them. As the last ones scurried up

to the water's edge, the goblins glanced at each other.

"We can get the shell piece now!" the biggest goblin shouted triumphantly. "Come on!"

"We must get back to Fairyland right away!" Tess cried, raising her wand.

There was a burst of golden sparkles and Rachel and Kirsty saw Pearl shrink down to fairy-size.

Then the four of them were whisked away on a cloud of fairy magic, leaving

the goblins standing on the beach, jumping up and down with rage.

A few seconds later, Tess, Rachel and Kirsty were back at the Royal Aquarium. Shannon, Ally, Amelie and Pia were waiting for them, all looking very excited. Pearl was already back in her tank of water, next to Echo the dolphin, Silky the seal and Scamp the penguin. The other Magical Ocean Creatures were thrilled to see Pearl back and they splashed around

in their tanks, calling out a greeting.

"That was close!" Tess said with a smile. "But we just made it!"

"Well done, all of you," Shannon beamed at them. "Now let's replace another missing piece of the Golden Conch Shell!"

Rachel handed her the fragment of shell.

Shannon walked over to the table where the pieces that had already been found were sitting on a golden stand. As Shannon held the shell piece out in front of her, there was a flash of dazzling light and the fragment sprang from Shannon's hand and fused magically with the other pieces, leaving no visible crack or join.

"Only three more pieces to find, and then our Golden Conch Shell will be whole once more!" Shannon said with delight. She turned to Rachel and Kirsty. "It's getting dark in Leamouth, so it's time to send you home, girls. Thank you again."

"Thank you," the fairies chorused as a shower of magical sparkles from Shannon's wand floated down around Rachel and Kirsty. "See you again soon!"

The girls waved goodbye and, a few seconds later, found themselves back on the beach in Leamouth near their sandcastle.

"Wasn't that an exciting fairy adventure, Rachel?" Kirsty sighed happily. Then she gave a gasp. "Look at our sandcastle!"

A beautiful silver flag, glittering in the last rays of the sun, had been placed on top of one of the towers.

"Fairy magic!" Rachel said happily. "I'm so glad we found another shell piece, Kirsty. And we helped all the baby sea turtles get safely into the ocean, too."

"Yes, and now it's time for us to go home!" Kirsty laughed, as they ran off

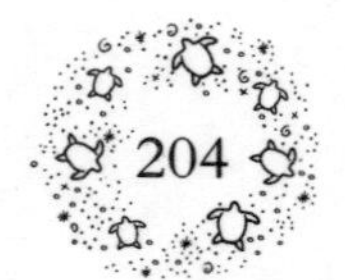

towards her gran's cottage. "The magic did come to us in the end, didn't it, Rachel? Even though it was a bit late in the day!"

Rachel nodded. "I hope we find another piece of the Magical Conch Shell tomorrow," she added. "Four found, three to go!"

The End

Discover all seven pieces of the Magical Conch Shell by reading the rest of the Ocean Fairies series

Find them all at rainbowmagicbooks.co.uk

Calling all parents, carers and teachers!
The Rainbow Magic fairies are here to help your child enter the magical world of reading. Whatever reading stage they are at, there's a Rainbow Magic book for everyone!

Read along the Reading Rainbow!

Well done – you have completed the book!

This book was worth 2 stars.

See how far you have climbed on the Reading Rainbow opposite.
The more books you read, the more stars you can colour in
and the closer you will be to becoming a Royal Fairy!

Do you want to print your own Reading Rainbow?

1) Go to the Rainbow Magic website

2) Download and print out the poster

3) Colour in a star for every book you finish
and climb the Reading Rainbow

4) For every step up the rainbow,
you can download your very own certificate

There's all this and lots more at

rainbowmagicbooks.co.uk

You'll find activities, stories, a special newsletter
AND you can search for the fairy with your name!